P9-BBP-858

HORSE DIARIES
·Maestoso Petra·

HORSE DIARIES

#1: *Elska*
#2: *Bell's Star*
#3: *Koda*
#4: *Maestoso Petra*

HORSE DIARIES

Maestoso Petra

JANE KENDALL

illustrated by RUTH SANDERSON

RANDOM HOUSE NEW YORK

This is a work of fiction. All incidents and dialogue, and all characters with the exception of some well-known historical and public figures, are products of the author's imagination and are not to be construed as real. Where real-life historical or public figures appear, the situations, incidents, and dialogues concerning those persons are fictional and are not intended to depict actual events or to change the fictional nature of the work. In all other respects, any resemblance to persons living or dead is entirely coincidental.

Text copyright © 2010 by Jane Kendall
Illustrations copyright © 2010 by Ruth Sanderson

Photo credits: © Associated Press (pp. 132–133); © Kolvenbach/Alamy (p. 138).

All rights reserved. Published in the United States by Random House Children's Books, a division of Random House, Inc., New York.

Random House and the colophon are registered trademarks of Random House, Inc.

Visit us on the Web! www.randomhouse.com/kids

Educators and librarians, for a variety of teaching tools, visit us at www.randomhouse.com/teachers

Library of Congress Cataloging-in-Publication Data
Kendall, Jane F.
Maestoso Petra / by Jane Kendall ; illustrated by Ruth Sanderson. — 1st ed.
p.   cm. — (Horse diaries ; 4)
Summary: Maestoso Petra, a Lipizzaner stallion, trains to perform in the Spanish Riding School and is hidden away during the German occupation of Austria in World War II.
ISBN 978-0-375-85842-0 (trade) — ISBN 978-0-375-95842-7 (lib. bdg.) — ISBN 978-0-375-89314-8 (e-book)
1. Lipizzaner horse—Juvenile fiction. 2. Spanische Reitschule (Vienna, Austria)—Juvenile fiction. [1. Lipizzaner horse—Fiction. 2. Spanish Riding School (Vienna, Austria)—Fiction. 3. Horses—Fiction. 4. Horsemanship—Fiction. 5. World War, 1939–1945—Austria—Fiction. 6. Austria—History—1938–1945—Fiction.]
I. Sanderson, Ruth, ill. II. Title.
PZ10.3.K32Mae 2010   [Fic]—dc22   2008039713

Printed in the United States of America

10 9 8 7 6 5 4 3 2 1

First Edition

Random House Children's Books supports the First Amendment and celebrates the right to read.

For Serena Du Bois

—J.K.

For Jane

—R.S.

CONTENTS

1
Home   1

2
Vienna   16

3
The Spanish Riding School   32

4
Music   49

5
War   64

❧ 6 ❦

Flight   77

❧ 7 ❦

Rescue   94

❧ 8 ❦

The Winter Riding Hall   110

❧ 9 ❦

Home   126

Appendix   131

"Oh! if people knew what a comfort to horses a light hand is . . ."
—from *Black Beauty*, by Anna Sewell

HORSE DIARIES
·Maestoso Petra·

Home

I am old now, but I have been young. And I remember.

I remember the Alpine meadows of my youth, where the grass was sweeter in the mouth than the lumps of sugar we were given as treats. I remember snow-topped mountains, so sharp against the bright blue sky I wondered if they were real. I remember learning to gallop on sturdy legs that changed month by month, as I watched in amazement, from black to gray to a smooth creamy white.

I remember the years of training that made me, step by careful step, into the perfectly mannered creature I became.

I remember war. I remember a sky turned red with fire, and the girl who whispered soothing words and fed me carrots stolen from her mother's soup pot. Her name was Liesl, and she always ran, her thick yellow braid bouncing down her back. I remember the soldiers who came to help us—tall, strong boys from America with loud voices and wide smiles and easy ways.

I am a Lipizzaner, proudly bred to dance the ancient steps, my hoofbeats silenced by the sawdust-covered floor of a gold and white ballroom. I remember the music, lilting and lovely, and the warming sound of applause. I remember it all.

But I should start, where all good stories start, at the beginning. I was born in 1932 at Piber, in the state of Styria in southeastern Austria. There the wheat fields stretch in waves of gold to the low brown hills and the mountains beyond, where the streams run icy with melted snow. We were all born there, my brothers and sisters and cousins, born in the lazy sunny years before the war.

I came at night. Josef, the stableman with the drooping mustache, held the lantern in

his trembling old hand, the dim light dancing around the walls of the stall where my mother lay. The first touch I felt was her soft muzzle and then her tongue, rasping and strong as she cleaned me. I stood . . . and then I fell to the straw, my legs folding under me, and old Josef laughed. I stood again, this time firmly, and I remember his voice saying, "A fine little Maestoso stallion. He should do well."

My name was decided at birth, as was the life I have led. I am called Maestoso Petra. My father was of the Maestoso line, which reaches back to the Spanish horses of Lipizza, and even further to the Arabians of the desert and the horses who carried the Romans into battle. Petra is for my mother. At first I stayed close to her, for I needed her warmth and comfort and milk, but soon she pushed me into the world beyond the foaling barn.

Go on, little one, said Mama Petra as she nudged me forward. *Feel the air on your face; taste the grass. Run!*

That first year I ran and ran, racing my brothers and sisters along the paddock railings. We nipped at each other's flanks to go faster,

faster, always faster. Sometimes important-looking men would come to watch us, leaning on the railing and talking in low voices.

In the spring I would see my mother guiding a new foal, as wobbly and coal black as I had once been, into the sunshine. *Another little brother or sister,* I would think, and wait for the time when they would find their legs and come to race me. Every summer we would leave our winter paddocks and be turned out to graze the high pastures. I remember the two grooms, Janni and Fritz, who led us up the long road into the mountains. They whistled and laughed as they strode along. That first year my mother and the other mares came, too. In the warm air that smelled of pine trees they would toss their heads and play with us. Those were happy times. I had no cares or even very many thoughts, nothing to do but race and eat and roll in a meadow dotted with white flowers, the sun warm on my back. The turf was soft and springy beneath my unshod hooves, and I would play and leap until the shadows grew long across the grass and it was time to go.

When I grew older I went up the mountain with just the stallions. Sometimes my father, Maestoso Elena, came with us. How proud I was to walk beside him and match my steps to his! Old horses like to talk about when they were young, and he told me of the wonderful things he had done in a city far away.

It is every Lipizzaner stallion's dream to go to Vienna, he said. *To be chosen for the Spanish Riding School is a great honor.*

Only stallions are chosen? I asked him.

Mares are not strong enough, he said seriously. *They cannot dance as we do, or fly through the air.*

That sounded very exciting! So I asked, a little shyly, if he thought I would be chosen.

Perhaps, he said, eyeing me. *You are light on your feet, and strong, and your coat is fading nicely.*

I was a medium gray by then, with a paler mane and tail. *When will I be white like you?* I asked.

Patience, Petra, patience, he said. *Only time will tell.*

At two I was branded. This sounds worse than it was, for it was done very quickly, in the blink of an eye. I remember standing in the courtyard of the main barn while the blacksmith heated his branding irons over glowing charcoal. Janni had a firm grip on my halter, and he kept patting my neck.

"This won't hurt, Petra," he said, patting away. "Honest. It's just that we have to know who you are all the time. And you can't exactly tell us, can you, boy?"

He was right. It didn't hurt, although the places did itch when they were healing. I have three brands. First is the *L* on my left cheek, which means I am a Lipizzaner—as if you couldn't tell by looking! On my left hindquarter there is a *P* under a small crown, because I was born at the Federal Stud at Piber. On my left side, where it's hidden by my saddle, is M for Maestoso. Under that is a squiggly line that means Mama Petra was descended from a great stallion named Pluto. I never thought about my brands until the frightening day I learned they could keep me from being stolen. Then I was quite glad I had them.

We were beautifully cared for, all of us treated like gold. Every night the straw in our stalls was freshly laid, the water in the bucket was always clean and cool, and the oats were fine and crisp with never a speck of chaff. We were groomed every day, too, brushed and curried until we shone like brass, our hooves picked clean and our manes and tails combed free of tangles. And while I liked the attention—I must say I liked it very much!—I wondered how my time in Piber would end. Would I go to Vienna, as my father and I hoped? *If you are not chosen in your fourth year, you will be sold. You could wind up in a* circus, he said, and snorted in disgust. *Or pulling a carriage. Or in the army.*

At the end of my fourth summer I found out. It was the close of a perfect afternoon. The barn swallows were chirping and calling as they darted in and out of the eaves. After he brushed me, Janni fastened a thick blue felt rug around me. We went out of the barn and across the courtyard to a large open truck with the back ramp let down. He led me to the ramp, and then I realized he wanted me to get in that thing. I didn't want to, so I balked and dug my feet into the dirt. But he put one strong hand on my flank and *pushed me*.

I was so surprised—Janni had never touched me any way but gently—that I skittered up the ramp before I knew what I was doing. He climbed in and fastened my rope to a ring on the side of the truck. Conversano Nina, a light dappled gray, had already been loaded into the truck, and he was breathing noisily and rolling his eyes.

"Be a good boy, my Petra. Be a good boy," Janni said in a husky voice. Then he ran back down the ramp, pulled it up, and fastened it to the back of the truck.

As we drove away I saw Mama Petra

standing at the paddock railing, her eyes so dark and liquid and loving. I wanted to break free and run to her and nuzzle against her as I hadn't for years. Then the truck turned onto the road that led to the town and I couldn't see her anymore.

The long journey to Vienna had begun.

Vienna

The road was narrow and dusty, no more than one lane of packed dirt. We went past fields of grain that were alive with bees, past whitewashed farmhouses and brown and white cows being driven home, their copper bells ringing in the twilight. (I didn't know the names of everything I was seeing, of course, but it was still pleasant to watch.) Once we passed a hay wagon that was pulled by a sad piebald horse with a long coat and shaggy feet. In between the farms the road wound through the forest, where the air was cool and damp and the shadows lay long and blue across the road. After an hour or so the road widened and we began to meet other trucks, and once an automobile honked its horn at us.

Then the farms ended and I began to see houses, and then more houses, and the road turned to pavement. Before I knew it we were rattling across a long stone bridge over the Mur River. By stretching my neck over the side of the truck, I could see the river, winding

wide and dark to the horizon. I could also see
a mountain and, on the top of it, a castle with
high walls and towers with pointed roofs like

witches' hats. All of this was
Graz, and it was the first
city I had ever seen.

We went through the center of town, through squares lined with old-looking houses with red tile roofs. Then we came to a building that took up an entire block. The truck turned down an alley at the end of the building. I began to hear the most frightful noises—grindings and clankings, and puffing, like the snorting of a giant beast—and I could see clouds of oily black smoke. Then we stopped, and the two men in the truck came around and let down the back ramp. Conversano Nina and I were led out of the truck, this time backward.

"Just in time," one of the men said. "I was worried we'd miss the train."

We came out of the alley onto a long concrete platform, with a roof made of hundreds of little glass panes that winked and flashed in the sunset. Lined up alongside this, stretching back as far as I could see, was a series of long cars all hitched together, with many doors and windows, gleaming with brass and shining green paint. Was this the train? At the very front the great black monster—the engine—was making all the grinding and clanking noises and spewing smoke. The platform was busy with men in uniform carrying suitcases, and people getting into the train and leaning out of the windows and calling *"Auf Wiedersehen!"* and waving their handkerchiefs.

Conversano Nina and I were led down the platform to the last car, which was not shiny green but was made of wooden slats like a barn. A small boy in knickers tugged at his mother's hand and said, "Look, Mama, such pretty horses!" One should always respond to a compliment, so I lifted my head and tossed my mane, and he laughed.

Then a stout, whiskery stationmaster in a blue uniform with brass buttons came running up to us. "Get those horses off my platform," he said angrily, waving a sheaf of papers under the nose of the man who held my halter. "I need them loaded, *now*."

"Calm yourself," said my man, and put a hand up. "All is in order, and someone will be along tomorrow morning to pick up the truck—"

"Truck?" the man sputtered, now quite red in the face. "What truck?"

"You don't think these horses flew here, do you?" said my man. "Although Lipizzaners have been known to leave the ground. You relax, Father," he said to the stationmaster. "All that matters is that we deliver these two fine boys to the *Spanische Reitschule*."

The *Spanische Reitschule*? I *had* been chosen! If my man hadn't been holding my halter so tightly, I would have leaped into the air and kicked up my heels!

"Why didn't you say so?" the stationmaster said. "That's a horse of a different color." Ah, he was all smiles now, chuckling at his own joke. "Right over there, and you will find the hay and feed all loaded for your trip."

So it was up another ramp (I was getting better at them) and into a stall with a good thick bed of straw. My man fastened a padded collar around my neck, which he tied to rings on the boxcar wall. He was a kind fellow, however, and left the rope loose so I could easily reach the manger in the corner. Then I heard the stationmaster yell, "All aboard!" A steam whistle sounded in a deafening shriek that flattened my ears against my skull, the floor jerked once, hard, underneath me, and we were on our way.

Conversano Nina was poor company throughout that long night, for he fretted and strained against his collar, his neck slick with lather. (I confess that by daybreak I had come to think of him as Conversano Ninny.)

I'm afraid, he cried. *I don't know what's happening.*

We are going to the Spanish Riding School,
I said proudly, but he didn't seem to hear me.
My papa says there is no finer honor. Still no
reply. *At least we have food and straw. Maybe
it will be an adventure.*

After a while I paid him no mind, for the
scene that unrolled beyond the open door of
the boxcar was as beautiful as anything I had
ever observed. As night fell, and then
passed, the train went through the villages
and farmlands of Styria, going north, north
to Vienna. I saw rivers tumbling over their
beds, and craggy cliffs outlined against the
stars. I saw tiny churches in mown fields, and
the bells in their white steeples swayed and
sang in the night wind.

Dawn came, the sky lifting to a pale

cloudless blue, and I saw houses painted in pink and blue and yellow, their window boxes blooming in purple and red, and market squares coming to life with mounds of vegetables and trays of round bread and flowers bright in pots. The wheels on the rails hummed a soothing rhythm, and the stations flicked by like scraps of paper on the breeze: Lassnitzhöhe, Bad Blumau, St. Johann Herberstein. Then up through the Vienna Woods, with its dark fir trees and ruined castles on the hills, the towns and taverns clustered along the tracks: Bad Schönau, Wiener Neustadt, Enzesfeld-Lindabrunn. Finally, the train slowed and we pulled into a station ·that was larger and grander than any we had passed. A loudspeaker crackled, "Südbahnhof—Wien!" and we were in Vienna.

Again Conversano Nina and I were led into a truck; again we were driven through a strange city. But this city was different—so large the buildings, so wide the streets! First we drove down Prinz Eugen Strasse, which ran beside a park with tall trees and winding paths. (I was pleased to see a number of handsome statues of horses with men on their backs.) After the train it felt good to be near trees and grass again, but everything was so tidy, so *groomed*. The paths were neat stripes of gravel and the flowers grew in rows like teeth. For a moment I longed for my Alpine meadow with the ragged sweet grass and the wildflowers, but then I shook off the thought. I was here, in the great city of Vienna, and I would make the best of whatever came my way. I might have been proud and foolish and young, but I was also determined.

Then we turned onto the Ring, a spacious avenue that made a two-and-a-half-mile circle through the heart of the city. Here was the Hofburg, the Imperial Palace that for centuries had been the winter home of the emperor, and the Parliament, with its grand steps like a Greek temple. Here was the State Opera House, and the grandest of grand hotels and the most fashionable shops and cafés. The Ring was many lanes wide, so wide that the streetcars ran both ways and there were little parks in the middle of the street.

And was it noisy! After my peaceful life in the countryside, not even the streets of Graz nor a night on a train had prepared me for the noise of a great European capital. It was constant, as never-ending as a river over stones, but, somehow, I liked it. I craned my neck to see over the side of the truck, to look at the Viennese. They strolled along the Ring talking and laughing and chatting, and sat gossiping at the café tables that spilled out onto the sidewalks. The city smelled of dust and stone and automobile exhaust— and I caught my first whiff of the rich aroma of coffee, for in those days Vienna was a city of coffee and coffeehouses. There was also a kind of snap to the air, like electricity. Surely, in a place like this, anything could happen.

The Spanish Riding School

My life truly began the morning after I arrived in Vienna. On that memorable day in August I began my training at the *Spanische Reitschule*, the Spanish Riding School. Here I would accomplish the purpose for which I had been chosen; here I would learn the dressage moves of the haute école, the high school, which I would perform all over the world.

I awoke in the roomy stall that would be my home for the next nine years. For the first time, I heard the bells of St. Stephen's Cathedral sweetly tolling the hours. The stables were in the vast complex of palaces and state buildings that made up the Hofburg—I was living in the Imperial Palace! We were just off the Josefsplatz in an old three-story building with steep slate roofs and many tall chimneys. The building was set well back off the street behind a large square courtyard, and wide covered walkways ran along the front of each story. It was very quiet, the noise of the city no more than a distant hum.

The Lipizzaners of the Spanish Riding

School were housed in two long rows of stalls on the first floor. (The offices and quarters for the *Oberbereiter*, the cavalry officers who trained us, and the *Bereiter*, our riders, were on the floors above.) I thought the barns at Piber were wonderful, but they were no match for the Stallburg. The ceiling was high and arched, and set into the carved molding over every stall was a graceful white statue of the head of a Lipizzaner. *Remember who you are*, they seemed to say. Although they were all cast from the same mold, I imagined that mine looked like Mama Petra, and I often spoke to her in those early days when I was feeling lonely. There were signposts at the front of each stall with our names on them, and our hay cribs were made of marble.

Whenever I was taken from my stall to be washed or exercised, I could see into the courtyard. It was very pleasant to gaze across the sun-washed cobblestones to the street and watch the delivery carts and automobiles, and the people passing by like characters in a play. In the evening the view was even prettier—especially, as I discovered that first winter, when the streetlamps were lit and the snow was falling in a silent blanket over the city.

Anton Knoedler was my groom, and a nicer fellow you never met. That first morning he came into my stall and introduced himself as he was brushing me. He ran his sturdy hands expertly over my hindquarters and announced, "A good strong boy you are, Maestoso Petra."

So I whinnied a little and nuzzled him, remembering my father's advice. *Listen to the humans*, Maestoso Elena had told me, *especially those who take care of you. You will never understand all they say—who does?—but they are important.*

"Ach!" Anton cried delightedly. "We will get on well. Time for Morning Parade now, so behave"—he wagged a forefinger at me—"and do as I say." After putting on a saddle blanket, he fastened a scarlet rug trimmed with gold braid around me. Then he took my halter and led me to the courtyard, where some twenty other Lipizzaner stallions were lined up, each with a groom at his head. The church bells chimed seven times. At an unseen signal, we all began to move forward.

As we came out to the Josefsplatz, the policeman who was directing traffic blew on his whistle, spread his arms, and screamed, "Halt!" Horns sounded, brakes squealed, and the traffic screeched to a stop.

The sidewalks were lined with the people who came every morning to watch us. Out of the corner of my eye I saw a little girl with round blue eyes push her way to the front of the crowd, her schoolbooks hugged to her chest. She stared at us with a kind of eager hunger on her face. Then the crowd shifted and I lost sight of her.

As we began to cross the street the most delicious aroma wafted into my nostrils, and I tried to turn my head to see where it was coming from.

Anton must have read my mind, for he grinned and said, "You smell that? It's the bakery on the corner." He lifted his head and sniffed, just like a horse. "*Apfel* strudel," he said happily. "Apples and sugar. Just what we like, eh?"

But there was no time to explore, for the parade was moving across the street and then across a wide plaza. We passed the statue of a Lipizzaner rearing, with Prince Eugène in the saddle, and then went under the grand archway that was the main entrance of the Hofburg. Another courtyard, a long hallway, and we had reached our destination—the Winter Riding Hall.

I had never seen anything like it, and to this day I think it the most beautiful place on earth. To say it was large is an understatement. It was *enormous*. It was flooded with light and as elegant as any ballroom you can imagine, with a high ceiling decorated with carvings and plaster moldings. Huge crystal chandeliers sparkled like waterfalls in the sunlight, which streamed in long, dusty beams through two stories of arched windows. The floor, which was covered by a thick layer of sand and sawdust, was twenty yards wide and sixty yards long. Around the walls were ranks of white pillars and behind those the galleries, where the Viennese came on Sunday mornings to watch us perform.

I was just a simple horse from the country, and I took one look and stopped short, my eyes wide and my sides heaving. Anton merely patted my rump and led me to the center of the floor. "You won't even notice after a while," he said to me. "You'll be too busy."

Within moments I found out what he meant. Martin Haas entered the hall with a saddle over one arm and all manner of gear looped over the other and came toward us. Martin was an *Oberbereiter*, a head rider. He was tall and slender, with close-cropped blond hair and an upright bearing that spoke of discipline and tradition. He was dressed in a dark brown jacket, breeches, and boots so polished you could see your reflection in them.

I saw that saddle over his arm and began to back up. Anton started stroking my neck and crooning words of comfort as he unbuckled my rug and slid it off my back. He knew what was coming.

Martin walked up to me, shifted the

weight in his arms, and stroked my muzzle. "This won't hurt, Maestoso Petra," he said gently. "I promise." Before I could think twice, he handed the looped reins and gear to Anton, slung the saddle onto my back, and bent down and buckled the girth around my stomach.

I am embarrassed now to admit such a thing, but I bucked. Oh, how I bucked! After a minute or two of jumping up and down and throwing out my feet—Anton and Martin wisely took a few steps back—I came down to earth and shook my head.

Puh, I thought with a snort. *This thing isn't going anywhere.* And it occurred to me, suddenly, that if this was what they wanted, it was a fair trade for a stall in a palace and for eating out of marble. So when Martin came at me with the bridle I stood quietly, as I tried to catch my breath and regain my dignity.

"See?" Martin said as he held the bit out to me. "So small." He lifted it and blew on it to warm the steel, and then swiftly slid it into my mouth. It felt odd for a moment, and then I decided it was no worse than the saddle. Then Martin clipped a twelve-foot-long rein called a longe to the bridle and took the free end in one hand. In his other hand he held a long whip, a thin six-foot strip of leather on a tall stick. And we began.

Martin backed up to the full length of the longe and started to turn slowly, so I was guided into making a circle around him.

Around I went in a measured circle, around and around for about three minutes, and then he let the longe go slack and said, "Halt." I halted.

"Excellent!" he exclaimed. He walked over to me, pulled a chunk of carrot out of the pocket of his jodhpurs, and held it under my mouth. That was more like it! I'd do just about anything for a sweet, crisp mouthful of carrot, so around and around we went for the rest of the morning: first walking, then, with a tiny flick of the whip—I was worried that it might sting but it tickled—he urged me into a slow trot. More circles, more carrots, and that was my first day in the Winter Riding Hall.

It was so exciting! I know that going

around in circles for hours doesn't sound exciting, but it was. It was thrilling. No longer was I watching the world slide by—I was *doing* something.

By the end of that first session I knew that my job was to please this tall blond man who spoke so softly and had such enticing treats in his pocket. I was coming to know the sound of his voice, and read from the subtle changes in tone when he was pleased and when he was not pleased. I knew that even if I was just going around in a circle, I should keep my head high and my neck arched and my steps even. I knew that this was the beginning.

Music

From that humble beginning I went forward, even though at first I thought nothing much was happening. Every morning the parade across the Josefsplatz; every morning the mouthwatering smells from the bakery and the little girl who took her place at the curb to stare at us; every morning my lessons with *Oberbereiter* Martin Haas. But an unchanging routine, I discovered, was the foundation of our work. Day by day little things were added, so gradually that I didn't realize how far I had come.

In those first months I was always on the longe. But I wore a saddle every day, so I would get used to the feel of it, and a full bridle. The reins were attached to my saddle to imitate the hands of a rider, which meant I could only move my head so far. Then came the day when Martin took off the longe and unfastened the reins. With a leg up from the faithful Anton, he swung easily onto my back, and off we went. We walked and then he gently urged me into a trot. I had been watching

the older and more experienced horses, and so I kept my steps even and strong and steady.

I could hear Anton clapping his hands as we came down the long side wall beneath the galleries. We reached the end of the hall, and Martin pulled me up, swung off, and gave me *two* chunks of carrot. "You're a fine student, Maestoso Petra," he said, pride warming his voice. "You are learning to obey, no matter what is asked of you."

Our training sessions were open to the public. I think this was so we would never be afraid of, or distracted by, an audience. The Viennese also liked to take tours of the Stallburg, and I got used to gentlemen in fur-collared coats and sweet-smelling ladies patting me as if I were a lapdog.

One afternoon a few months after my arrival, the girl from Morning Parade suddenly appeared at the stables. She walked right in and came up to Anton, who was standing in the aisle with brush in hand, about to start my daily grooming.

"Liesl!" he exclaimed. "Liesl Haas! What are you doing here?"

"I have come to be with the horses," she said firmly. "I was nine years old yesterday, and Papa says I'm old enough to know how to behave. That was my special birthday treat," she added anxiously. "To be allowed to come here. I won't be a bother, honest."

That was how Martin's daughter came into my life, as simply and as naturally as could be. I still have no idea why she took such a liking to me, but I'm glad she did. Maybe she felt a kinship because we were both young and green. Or maybe she knew that even though Anton groomed five other horses, I was his favorite, and she wanted to please him. Liesl followed Anton like a shadow, and he answered her stream of questions seriously and with great patience. He also showed her how to clean my tack with saddle soap and a rag, which she did quite well. They would sit together outside my stall and chatter away about saddles and snaffle bits and who was the best Lipizzaner of all time.

I came to think of Liesl as *my* girl. Every day she would wiggle her fingers at me during Morning Parade, and I would nod my head (that was our secret signal). Every afternoon she appeared as soon as school let out for the day. She wore her school uniform, her knees poking out between the pleated skirt and prickly knee socks. She would toss her schoolbooks into a corner with a kind of glee, followed by the ugly round hat that left a red mark on her forehead when she tore it off. "I'm here!" she would sing out.

Always polite—Liesl was the daughter of a cavalry officer, after all—she would greet the other horses before she came to my stall. Then, quickly looking to see if anyone was about, she would slip me the treat of the day: grainy brown lumps of her mama's coffee

sugar, pale-green stalks of celery with the leaves on, and, best of all, fat red apples brimming with juice.

And so life settled into the routine that would continue, unbroken, for years: peaceful afternoons with Anton and my girl, busy mornings with Martin. At one end of the hall, two six-foot-high wooden pillars were set into the floor some four feet apart. Here, tied between the pillars, we practiced the most difficult moves—moves that were intricate and demanding, and had to be learned from a standing position. The long whip was used to tickle us into moving one leg or the other as our *Oberbereiter* wished, over and over again; at the same time we would be given a vocal command or a twitch on the bit. This was our introduction to the haute école. When we could do the move without the flicking whip, we would take our new skills out onto the floor—first on the longe or two long reins, and finally with a *Bereiter*.

How I longed to leave the pillars and try my legs! How I longed to be like Conversano Stornella, with his noble head and grave manner, or Favory Montenegro, with his clever, fast feet. How I longed to try the "shouldering in," where the horses moved on the diagonal so smoothly that they seemed to float over the floor. Or the *piaffe*, which looks simple and is anything but—a fiery standing trot that is so precise, so intense, that I could barely breathe the first time I was taken through it.

The most amazing were the "airs above the ground," the dramatic moves only Lipizzaner stallions can do. (I was somewhat annoyed to hear Anton tell Liesl that this was not because we were more intelligent than other breeds, but because of the way we were built.) To see Conversano Stornella rear into the *levade*, and then hold the pose while time stood still before dropping lightly to the floor, was thrilling. How I loved to see him do the *courbette*, where he balanced on his hind legs before hopping forward. Or watch Favory Montenegro leap into the *croupade* with his legs tucked up under him—and then take it one step further to the *capriole*, where he kicked out his hind legs midjump! I lived for the day when I could fly into the air as they did. Would I ever be able to learn—or perfect—such magnificent and important moves?

In those first months I was taught to bow, striking out my right hoof and lowering my head over it. This was so I could pay my respects to the emperor Charles VI, who had founded the Spanish Riding School in 1735. His portrait, which almost covered the back wall of the imperial box, was the one spot of bright color in the glittering white hall. Every Lipizzaner bows to him on entering and leaving the Winter Riding Hall, for where would we be without him?

On a frosty Sunday morning when the air smelled like snow and my breath puffed white from my nostrils, I made my debut. Not happily trotting as I had with Martin, but walking on the longe. Before the performance that day, Conversano Nina and I were to be led around the hall, just one quick circuit to introduce the new horses to the public. *I'm almost white now*, I thought as I looked down at my legs, where only a little gray remained around my hooves. *At least I'll* look *like a real performer*. . . .

All the little gilt chairs in the galleries were filled. The emperors were long gone, so the mayor sat in the imperial box with men from the parliament and their richly dressed wives. As Martin and I entered and I prepared to make my bow, I heard the most enchanting sound. It was like birds, or maybe wind through the trees, and there was a rhythm to it that made my ears twitch and my feet want to move.

I must have reacted, for Martin smiled.

"You like the music?" he whispered to me. "That's Mozart, the *Eine kleine Nachtmusik*. He was a good Austrian, just like us."

Oh! It was lovely, even from two violins, a viola, and a cello. Years later we would have a full orchestra with French horns and flutes, but I still remember those four musicians and the magic they made. I found myself matching my steps to the delightful rhythm and melody that seemed to pull me along and make my hooves skim lightly over the floor. And that's when I realized that nothing we Lipizzaners did was meant to be done in silence or to a voice counting out beats. We were not mechanical toys that marched along without a soul—we were *dancers*.

From that moment on I was like Pegasus, a horse with the white feathered wings of an angel. Every step I took, no matter how simple, was fueled by the music I heard in my head, which spurred me on.

War

In 1938 our troubles began. It was a frightening year, for many things changed . . . and if there's one thing horses hate, it's change. We like to eat the same things every day and sleep in the same stall every night, and we don't like it when the people who take care of us are unhappy.

In March of that year, my country was taken over. The Anschluss, it was called, a hissing sort of word that meant that we were now part of Germany. The Republic of Austria—my beloved Austria of the snow-capped mountains and golden wheat fields—was no more. Our lives would be ruled by the Nazis in Berlin and by Adolf Hitler, who was the chancellor of Germany. He was known as the Führer, the leader—a phrase spoken with pride by those who thought he was the answer to all their problems, and whispered in fear by those who knew better. We were, I now know, luckier than the poor people of Poland or Belgium or France, who would be invaded by the German army over the following two years, but it still made me sad.

I didn't know war was coming; I didn't even know what the word meant. I just knew that suddenly everyone around me started acting nervous and afraid. The first hint that something was wrong came on the twelfth of March, the day of the Anschluss. For the first time in memory there was no Morning Parade to the Winter Riding Hall. We stayed in the Stallburg for the next three days, straining our ears to the noises coming from the city outside: heavy boots marching in the streets, the loud grinding rumble of tanks and trucks rolling along the Ring, and people cheering. Every time we heard cheering Anton would make a face as if he were eating a lemon and mutter, "Sheep. They're no better than sheep."

On the fifteenth of March Liesl came dashing in, her cheeks flushed and her hat on crooked. She said hundreds of thousands of people were gathered in the Heldenplatz, the vast Heroes' Plaza in front of the Parliament. Adolf Hitler had come down from Berlin to hold one of his famous rallies.

"Führer, my foot," said Martin, who was spending the afternoon with Anton. "There's nothing worse than a failed artist."

"Shhh, Papa, no!" Liesl whispered, her eyes wide with fear. "It's not safe to say such things."

"Trust me, *Liebchen*," he said. "If the man could have made a living as a painter, we wouldn't be in this mess."

"Is it bad, Papa? I mean, *really* bad? Will the Nazis close the school?"

"Of course not," said Anton stoutly.

"I'm guessing they don't care what we do, as long as we don't make waves," said Martin. "Thank heavens we are so far from Berlin. Besides," he said teasingly, "if they close the *Reitschule* we'll have to take your brother right to the hospital, eh?"

Liesl said nothing but I knew this was a sore subject: her brother, Hans, after years of pleading and waiting, had just started to train as a *Bereiter*, continuing the Haas family tradition into the fifth generation. Liesl was tall for her eleven years and Hans short for his sixteen, and they looked so alike that from the back you could only tell them apart by her braid.

And Liesl, with a yearning that was written on her face every time she looked at a Lipizzaner, wanted to be a *Bereiter*.

"But you know how it is," Anton said to her. "Only stallions are trained; only men can ride them. No girl has ever been a *Bereiter*."

"What has *that* to do with anything?" she replied angrily. "Papa's been giving me riding lessons in the park since I was seven. I'm *good*. I never jerk the bit and I understand horses. It's not fair."

"Ach, I remember those days," Anton said wistfully. "When I was so young I thought life was fair."

The Heldenplatz emptied, Hitler went back to Berlin, and my days returned to normal. But the ground had shifted under my hooves, and somehow I didn't feel safe. People had started to disappear. Sweet old Herr Epstein, who sold hand-carved wooden toys from a little cart on the Josefsplatz—gone. One day he was there and the next he wasn't, and I never saw him again. Liesl would come in from school with stories of friends who had simply vanished, and no one ever asked what had happened to them.

In the midst of all the tension and sadness,

something wonderful happened to the Spanish Riding School. On New Year's Day of 1939 we were placed under the control of the Wehrmacht, the German Armed Forces. When I first heard about this, I wondered if I would have to join the cavalry and fight in battles! It only meant we could go on as before, since the important generals in Berlin, the capital of Germany, thought we were a tradition worth preserving. But the best of all was that Count van der Straten, who was the head of the school, retired. I don't mean to sound as if I didn't like him— he was a fine fellow with lovely manners— but he was old and tired, and running the school was no easy task.

Colonel Alois Podhajsky was named the new *Rittmeister*. The day he came striding into the Winter Riding Hall should be celebrated every year with parties and apples and fireworks! Without the Colonel (that was how I always thought of him), the Spanish Riding School would not have survived. Without the Colonel, I would never have performed for a great American general or seen the world. But I'm getting ahead of my story. . . .

I remembered the Colonel from my first year in Vienna; he had been a *Bereiter* for two years before the army decided he should train cavalry officers instead. The Colonel was a splendid rider who had competed in dressage events at the 1936 Olympic Games in Berlin. He was tall and handsome, with a long, lined face and dark hair that, as soon as he took over the school, seemed to grow grayer by the day.

There is an old saying that a new broom sweeps clean. That was the Colonel. He turned every inch of the Stallburg inside out, poking into corners and cleaning out drawers and cupboards. He even found the money to freshen the Winter Riding Hall, which badly needed a coat of paint and much dusting and scrubbing. It was he who decided that we should have an orchestra, and he who combed Vienna for the finest unemployed musicians. He put old horses and old *Bereiter* out to pasture and brought up new horses from Piber and new *Bereiter* from his old cavalry unit. The Stallburg hummed like a beehive, and on Sundays there was a line waiting to get into the Winter Riding Hall.

He made one change that brought the widest smile I had ever seen to Anton's face. Ever since the Anschluss, the *Bereiter* had been told to thank the people for their applause by raising their right arms stiffly, in the Nazi salute. "It is a monstrosity," said the Colonel. "No more." So the *Bereiter* went back to lifting their cocked hats with a flourish, as they had for two centuries. That was when I knew the Colonel was a brave man who cared more about the Spanish Riding School than anyone ever had.

It was all so exciting, and we were all so busy, that it was almost—*almost*—possible to forget that Europe was at war. And the war was coming closer.

Flight

To this day I'm not sure how the Colonel kept the Spanish Riding School going through the war. Maybe he just pretended that nothing had changed. On the surface that was how it looked, for Morning Parade and training sessions and performances continued as before.

But Vienna was a gloomy place. You almost never saw men in the streets anymore, unless they were too young or too old to be soldiers. Instead of the jolly policeman, a woman in a long coat and shabby boots directed traffic in the Josefsplatz. No more the rich aroma of coffee wafting out of sidewalk cafés or *Apfel* strudel smells from the bakery. The Viennese lined up every morning with their ration cards, waiting for dark heavy bread made from rough flour, and by midday even that was gone.

Somehow the Colonel kept our *Bereiter* and grooms from being sent away to fight. He even persuaded the Wehrmacht to send us straw and hay and grain every month. As the war went on it was longer and longer between shipments, and sometimes the hay was moldy. The oats were awful.

And no more treats from Liesl. No more squares from her mama's sugar bowl, for sugar was rationed and in short supply. No more celery and no more apples, and the carrots she brought me were tough and wrinkled.

"I'm sorry, Petra," she said mournfully. "It's the best I can do. Mama wanted these for the soup, but I won't eat much tonight." She gave me a potato once. I didn't want to hurt her feelings, so I ate it, but there's nothing very nice about a raw potato.

On the brighter side, I had completed my training! Now I performed in the Sunday-morning exhibitions, which followed a strict order. We entered in single file and went

through our various gaits, including the
piaffe, and then came the grand quadrille,
where we crisscrossed the hall in complex
and wonderful patterns. We ended with the
"airs above the ground," which were always
greeted with gasps of awe. It had taken years
of strain and sweat and practice, but I had

learned my two (the airs are so difficult that most Lipizzaners can only master two). After Martin and I had tried all of them, he had decided which moves I did the most easily and gracefully. And so I performed the levade and the courbette I had dreamed about as a young horse. To rear into the perfect pose and

then jump forward on my hind legs—two, three, four, *five* times—was all I had ever wanted. Maybe I was showing off a little, but it was my favorite part of every performance.

I always smiled to myself when the new horses from Piber were led around the hall on the longe. I knew they watched me every morning, as I had once watched Conversano Stornella and Favory Montenegro. *Do you keep the music in your heads?* I asked them. *Does it make you want to dance?* I hoped they were inspired, as I had been. Dancing to Mozart and Strauss, and hearing the people of Vienna reward us with their applause, was what kept us going in those years. We made them forget their troubles, if only for an hour, and that is a job worth doing.

Every summer we left the Stallburg to stay at the Schönbrunn, the imperial summer palace in the town of Lainz. It was deep in the Vienna Woods, and we could graze on the lawn. After the food the Wehrmacht had been sending us, it was wonderful to taste real grass, but it was an eerie place. The lawn was surrounded by looming fir trees that blotted out the sun, and at night, when all was quiet, I could hear the lions in the Lainz Zoo. I was always glad when summer ended and we returned to the Stallburg.

In the summer of 1944 the bombing of Vienna began. How I longed then to be *anywhere* else, even if it was dark and spooky and lions roared at me. But the Colonel was afraid the wooden stables of the Schönbrunn would not protect us like the stone walls of the Stallburg, and so we stayed in the city. Anton had always said that the Allies, the English and Americans who were trying to free Europe from the Nazis, would never bomb Vienna. "They did not bomb Paris or Rome," he told me, "and Wien is every inch as old and historic and beautiful." I wish he had been right.

Airplanes flew low over the city, great roaring birds that made the air tremble like a thunderstorm. From their bellies fell bombs, which exploded with huge *bangs!* that made the ground shake and buildings fall down. At night we listened for the wailing sirens, which meant the airplanes were coming. That was the signal to file out of our stalls and into the courtyard for what Anton cheerfully called Evening Parade. The Winter Riding Hall was a strong building with thick walls, and it became the air-raid shelter for the Lipizzaners and the people in our neighborhood. One raid in September lasted for over an hour, and all the windows broke and the doors came off their hinges.

"You are such a smart boy, Petra," said Anton, who never left my side. "So brave, so quiet." It's true—I was quiet. When the noise got very loud and the floor wouldn't stop shaking, I put my head between my legs and remembered meadows and apples and clear blue skies while I waited for it to stop. I wanted to run, but why even try? There was nowhere to go.

After that September raid, the Colonel had everything packed up: the uniforms and the perky cocked hats of the *Bereiter*; the framed pictures of past Lipizzaners on the walls; our everyday tack; and the double bridles that were decorated with gold leaf, the soft handmade saddles, and the fringed scarlet saddle blankets we wore to perform. He even had the great crystal chandeliers in the Winter Riding Hall taken down from the ceiling and packed into crates.

Even though the Colonel made us exercise and train every morning, our performances had stopped in May. It was too dangerous for people to walk through Vienna, even to see my courbette. The Colonel also went away for days at a time, hitching rides on ammunition trucks into Upper Austria, trying to find a place far away where we would be safe. It was more than the bombing, said Anton; the Russians were moving in from the east, and everyone was afraid of the Russian army.

We left Vienna on the sixth of March, almost six years to the day since the Anschluss. The year before, a rumor had swept through the city that the Spanish Riding School was being shipped off to Berlin. It wasn't true, but the people of Vienna had gathered at the Stallburg to protest loudly and unhappily. I guess the Colonel didn't want to cause more trouble, so we left in the middle of the night, when everyone was asleep. Again I was loaded into a truck and driven through the streets, this time past piles of rubble and houses torn in two, past more destruction and misery than I could bear. A train was waiting for us at the Franz Josefs Bahnhof. It was no shining green creature like the one that had brought Conversano Nina and me to Vienna, but a battered wreck that sputtered and coughed and stank. But Anton was with me, and my girl. (Martin had begged the Colonel to let Liesl and her mama come along, and the Colonel had agreed.)

The boxcar was drafty and crowded with too many horses, and there was only a thin layer of filthy straw to stand on. There were many stops and starts. Every time we pulled into another bomb-damaged station, the Colonel would have to argue with the station-master and show his travel orders from

Berlin before we could be on our way. The train didn't go very fast, and it shuddered along as if the wheels were square instead of round.

We went west, away from Vienna, and the night was bitter cold. Through the open door I could once again smell the sharp scent of pine trees and see rivers tumbling over their beds. The night wind sang sweetly over the rattle of the train. We were going into the mountains, and my heart seemed to lift with every mile.

We made it as far as Wels before the airplanes came back.

They came in wave after wave, at night and in the daylight, and the sky turned red and filled with smoke as the fine old city burned.

The train pulled into the station at Wels and there we stayed for *two and a half days*. Horses are more afraid of fire than anything—you never know where it will go next—and Anton and Liesl and Hans, who had bravely walked back along the tracks to help us, had their hands full keeping us calm. By the second day we were even a little bored. There was nothing to do, nothing to eat or drink. And so we waited.

On the tenth of March we finally reached our destination: St. Martin im Innkreis, a tiny old-fashioned village built around the foot of a castle. We arrived at dusk. The lady who owned the castle greeted us as graciously as if we had arrived in fine carriages for a party, not rattling up the hill in trucks.

War had not been kind to the castle. It was as dirty and tired as we were. The stables were a mess. The wooden walls between the stalls had been used for firewood by the Polish and Russian prisoners of war who lived in the castle and worked the farms in the valley. So we stayed in the cowsheds while the Colonel found wood—some of it cut from the forest—and had it made into new walls. Fresh straw was put down, and we were fed and watered and left for the night.

There is no other way to say this. We ate those walls . . . and they were *delicious*. If you've ever tasted a fresh sapling, all green and tender with a thin, crispy crust of bark, you won't blame us a bit. After years of no apples and dried-up carrots, it was a thrill to tear into something crunchy! Once the walls were down we did have a party, waltzing around in the fresh straw and stretching our legs and poking into corners and nipping each other.

When the Colonel saw the next morning what we had done, he just laughed and made new walls, which he painted with something that made them taste terrible. We were there to stay, at least for a while.

Rescue

I thought St. Martin would be safe, but nowhere was truly safe in the spring of 1945. Airplanes streaked over the valley, and we could hear the deep rumble of artillery to the west. The American army was moving down through Germany and into Austria, liberating towns and villages and fighting what was left of the Nazi empire.

Although the castle was large, with more than fifty horses, our *Bereiter* and grooms, and hundreds of prisoners of war and refugees, it was dreadfully crowded. There was only one small shed to train in, and we certainly couldn't stay in our stalls all day and grow fat and lazy. So the Colonel decided we should put on our everyday tack and go hacking about the countryside, just like normal horses. But there were more horses than *Bereiter*. Thus, after the Colonel tested her skills (and Martin put in a good word), Liesl was allowed to ride me. You can imagine how excited we were!

There is nothing more peaceful and pleasant than spring in the mountains. The air was soft and cool, the trees were covered with new leaves, and pink and yellow wild-flowers grew beside the trails that wound into the hills. Every time you came around a curve, you could see the farms in the valley below, spread out like a green and brown patchwork quilt, or the breathtaking line of mountains to the east.

"If you pretend those artillery guns are thunder," Liesl said to me one afternoon as we rode along, "it could almost be the old days, before the war."

But it wasn't, and that was a dangerous thing to forget.

It was a perfect April day, and we were heading into the forest. There was a thick cushion of pine needles on the trail, which reminded me happily of the floor in the Winter Riding Hall. The birds were cheeping and peeping and flying around, and squirrels chattered in the trees. I was ambling along, daydreaming, when suddenly Liesl cried out and pulled me up short.

Two German soldiers stood in front of us. Their uniforms were ragged and dirty. The younger one had a bloodstained bandage on his forehead, just below his helmet.

"Oh ho, what have we here?" said the older of the two. "A fine lady on a fine horse. You better give me that horse, lady."

"I can't do that," said Liesl. Her voice was calm but her hands were shaking on the reins.

"You don't argue with me," he growled,

and then he grabbed the gun stuck in his belt and *pointed it at us*.

"This is a Lipizzaner; he belongs to the state." Now her voice was shaking, too. "If you steal him you'll go to prison."

"All I see is a horse I can sell," he said angrily, and gestured with the gun. "Down. Off."

"Look at his head," Liesl said loudly. "See the brand, the *L*? He's *famous*. You'll never get away with it. See?" She pulled my right rein sharply so he could see my left cheek. I knew it was really so I could start to turn around. Then she gave me a mighty kick with both heels and we were off!

I hadn't galloped since my days in the meadow and I put everything into it. I *flew*

down that trail so fast I don't think I touched the ground half the time, and Liesl was light in the saddle. I could hear footsteps pounding behind us. After a while they stopped, but we didn't! I burst out of the forest like a racehorse coming down the homestretch, sped across a field, and clattered into the courtyard in front of the castle. I was panting and my sides were heaving and Liesl was screaming, "Men, men in the forest!"

That was the end of afternoon rides.

By May the artillery was very loud, roaring like the lions in the zoo. Anton told me the end of the war was only days away. The village of St. Martin erupted into panic. The Americans were coming, and no one knew what they would do. Would they burn down the village, or put everyone in prison? Would they make life worse than it already was? People broke into the bakery and the greengrocer's to steal food. The road past the castle was filled with exhausted German soldiers and frightened villagers trying to get away. Somehow, in the midst of all this, the Colonel found ordinary clothing for the *Bereiter* to wear instead of their Wehrmacht uniforms. They were fine riders and not Nazis, and he wanted the Americans to know that.

The Americans arrived at the castle on May 2, 1945, pulling up in a fleet of funny green cars with no tops called jeeps. The Colonel went out to meet them. He was the *Rittmeister* of the Spanish Riding School of Vienna, he explained, and not a Wehrmacht officer to be arrested and put in prison. But the general who was in charge of the Twentieth Army Corps had never heard of the Spanish Riding School! There was only one thing to do. We had to show the Americans who, and what, we were.

Just four days later, with almost no rehearsal, we gave the performance on which our future would depend. Instead of a hall, we were in an open field. Along one side, seats were set up for all the American generals in the area; the troops in their baggy green uniforms and muddy boots stood or sat on the ground on the other three sides. The generals filed in, looking very important with decorations and medals shining on their chests and gold braid on their hats.

The last one to come in was a four-star general named George Patton. When the Colonel saw him, I think he relaxed a bit, since General Patton was a famous horseman who had also competed in the Olympic Games. "It's a good sign," Martin whispered to me as we waited for everyone to sit down.

We began with a pas de deux, two horses moving as one, and Martin and I shouldered in beside the Colonel and Pluto Theodorosta, who was his favorite mount. Out of the corner of my eye I could see that General Patton was somewhat bored, since he kept turning to chat with the generals on either side of him. Then we went into the best piaffe I have *ever* done . . . and he stopped talking. By the time we got to the levades

and the caprioles and my courbette, he was leaning forward and smiling.

When we finished and bowed—to General Patton instead of the emperor—everyone went wild! The generals clapped and clapped. The soldiers, the big strong boys from America, yelled and stomped their feet and put their fingers in their mouths and whistled like steam engines. I heard one soldier with freckles and red hair say, "Those are the smartest horses I ever did see." I had to bow four times. When everyone was finally quiet, the Colonel dismounted and made a speech, thanking the Americans for honoring us with their presence. Then he asked for their help: for us, and for the Federal Stud.

I did not know then—how could I?—

that although the Lipizzaners of Vienna had found refuge, the Lipizzaners of Piber had not. The Nazis had taken them from Styria to a town called Hostau, in the north in Czechoslovakia. When they started to lose the war and ran out of food for the horses, they set them loose. They drove them into the mountains of Czechoslovakia and left them there. All the gentle mares and the proud stallions, driven into the wilderness to fend for themselves.

It's a good thing I didn't know this until later, for I never would have been able to sleep for worrying. But General Patton did help. He sent a fleet of small airplanes up over the mountains to see where the horses had gone. Then he found soldiers who had grown up on ranches in Montana and Wyoming, cowboys from the great American West, and had them round up those horses and bring them back. It took days. I am ashamed to say that many of the stallions kicked and bit and behaved as if they had no manners. They didn't want to be loaded into trucks by men they had never seen, but the soldiers didn't give up. Those wonderful American boys rescued more than two hundred Lipizzaners.

The horses were brought to St. Martin so the Colonel could look them over and make sure they were healthy. The stallions were put into one paddock, the mares into another. And one day when Anton was taking me for a little exercise, just on a rope and bridle to walk the kinks out of my legs, I saw the mares.

They looked more like wild horses than the finely bred mares of Piber. Their manes and tails were snarled and tangled with burrs and brambles, and they were so thin you could count their ribs. As they milled about the paddock, politely taking turns at the water trough and the bales of hay, one of them caught my eye. There was something about her—something that called out to me across the years—and so I whinnied, and then I neighed as loudly as I could.

Mama! Mama Petra, is it you?

At first nothing . . . and then she wearily lifted her head and looked at me. There was a tiny flicker of recognition in her dark eyes, and then she tossed her head and whickered and pushed her way to the fence.

I am here, little one, she cried. *I am here.*

I pulled so hard on the rope that Anton had no choice but to follow. My mama, my Petra, stretched her neck over the top rail and we rubbed our heads together, stroking and nuzzling each other and making little contented noises in our throats.

There have been many fine and important moments in my life, but that was the sweetest.

The Winter Riding Hall

After the war we went to live in Wels, the city I had seen in flames from the train. The cavalry barracks and their stables had survived. That must have pleased the Colonel, who had trained there as a young officer. My mother and her sisters stayed in St. Martin until they were fit to travel, and then went home to Piber. I never saw Mama Petra again. But I knew she would be fed and loved, and that was all I could hope for.

Liesl and her mother went back to Vienna, so Liesl could finish her schooling and go to the university. The day they left she hugged me as if she never wanted to let go, and my neck was wet with her tears. "*Auf Wiedersehen*, my Petra," she whispered. "We'll be together again, I promise."

When we had left Vienna in March of 1945, we thought it would be for a short time. But the Colonel went there soon after the war ended and came back with terrible stories. The city was in ruins. Entire blocks were gone, and pieces of houses stuck up from the rubble like broken teeth. The Stallburg had been hit by bombs and was badly damaged. The Winter Riding Hall had been spared, but it was being used to store crates and scenery from the State Opera House, which had also been bombed. No more Vienna Woods—the stables of the Schönbrunn had burned to the ground, just as the Colonel had feared. Vienna was lost to us.

It takes money to feed horses and people, and we had no money. So we took to the open road, like a troupe of actors traveling from one village to the next. Liesl's brother, Hans, was my *Bereiter* now, and Martin stayed in Wels to train the new horses. After the story of how the Lipizzaners had been rescued by the American soldiers spread around the world, everyone wanted to see us. I remember a stadium in Switzerland with lovely, firm turf, and the riding hall of Christiansborg Palace in Copenhagen, as elegant as my Winter Riding Hall but smaller. We gave a special exhibition at the 1948 Olympic Games, and for the president of Italy in the historic medieval piazza of Siena. We even danced for Queen Elizabeth II of England, who is quite fond of horses. We sailed on a ship all the way to America to perform in Madison Square Garden. One of the New York City newspapers said we were better dancers than the Rockettes, whoever they were.

It was all very exciting . . . but I missed my stall, with the Lipizzaner statue gazing serenely down at me and the sounds of the

Josefsplatz wafting across the courtyard. I missed the way the sunlight streamed through the windows of the Winter Riding Hall, and the aromas of coffee and *Apfel* strudel in the streets. And I missed my girl.

I was not to see Vienna for ten years. Finally, in the autumn of 1955, the Stallburg was rebuilt and the Winter Riding Hall was restored so we could return. I was an old horse by then, but we Lipizzaners can perform well into our twenties and we often live into our thirties. I liked to think that I was still in my prime, and so I was ready—I was eager!—for whatever came next.

When our train pulled into the *Südbahnhof*, a band was playing and a large crowd was waiting, with newspaper reporters and television and newsreel cameras. And there was Liesl, at the very front of the crowd, calling my name over and over again and holding up a bag of apples! She looked all grown-up, but her long braid still shone down her back, and her round blue eyes were as sparkly and friendly as ever.

The next morning, when we came out of the Stallburg for Morning Parade, the Viennese clapped and cheered, so happy were they to see us again. As we walked down the street they would shyly reach out to touch us or stroke our manes—just to make sure we were real and not a dream from the past— and many were smiling and weeping at the same time. We had left in secret and returned in triumph!

I slipped back into the old routine as easily as slipping into a well-worn bridle: mornings in the Winter Riding Hall with Martin, who was back from Wels to correct any bad habits I had picked up on tour, and afternoons with my girl. The only thing missing was Anton, who had retired to a little cottage in Wiener Neustadt. My days seemed odd without him, but every Sunday he took the train up to comb my tail and bring me carrots from his garden.

I worked harder in those weeks than I ever had, preparing for the grand gala on October 14, 1955, that would mark the reopening of the Winter Riding Hall. Hans came early that night—he always liked to check the tack and be with me for a few minutes while it was quiet—and Liesl came to wish us luck. They were both in such high spirits that they started waltzing around my stall. And that's when Hans tripped over my water bucket . . . and went down, hard.

He sat up in the straw, clutching his right ankle and rocking back and forth and moaning.

"Hansie, what is it?" Liesl said worriedly. "Are you all right?"

"Take my boot off," he panted, and put his right leg out. Liesl tugged and pulled and got it off, and then gasped and put a hand over her mouth. His right ankle was bright red and already so swollen and puffed you couldn't see the anklebone. "That's it," he said miserably. "Go tell Colonel Podhajsky we'll be a horse short. Unless he's got a spare *Bereiter* in his pocket."

"Why can't Papa ride Petra?"

"Then who would ride Neapolitano Afrika?"

"You *have* to ride!" she cried. "Petra *has* to perform in the gala."

So he struggled to his feet and tried to

walk. "No good," he said after two painful steps. "I'll never get my foot into the stirrup. Or get my boot back on, for that matter. I'm sorry, Liesl." He reached out and patted my neck. "Poor Petra. It looks like you've got the night off."

"Then there's only one thing to do," Liesl said with a strange gleam in her eyes. She dashed to the tack room and was back in seconds with a large pair of scissors. With one sharp *snick*, her braid slithered down her back and curled into the straw at my feet like a shining yellow snake.

"What are you doing?" Hans said, staring at her.

"I'm going to ride Petra."

That started quite an argument! In the

end, however, Hans had no choice but to agree. "I must be crazy," he kept muttering. "This will never work." They hid in a supply closet to change clothes, Hans back into his suit and tie and Liesl into his uniform: beige breeches and boots that came up over the knee (the feet were too big, so she stuffed the toes with handfuls of my hay), a special scarlet tailcoat for the gala, and spotless white gloves. The black cocked hat was the finishing touch. It sat snugly on her head, with two little wings over the ears, like handles.

"How do I look?" she asked as he gave her a leg up into my saddle.

"Not bad," he said gruffly.

"I know I can do this, Hansie. I know it."

"Ah, this old boy knows the routine so well he could do it in his sleep," said Hans as he stroked my muzzle. "Just don't fall off and you'll be all right. But keep your head down and *don't* look anyone in the face. If you get me fired, I'll never speak to you again. And Papa will kill us both."

The Winter Riding Hall never looked more splendid than it did on that crisp fall night. Every crystal in the chandeliers had been washed and polished so they cast rainbows around the white walls and the carved ceiling. There was a new layer of sand and sawdust on the floor, with two dates lettered in pale yellow sawdust against the brown: 1735, when the *Spanische Reitschule* was founded, and 1955, when we came home.

The galleries were packed, not an empty seat to be had, and people were standing in the back against the windows. The men were in evening clothes, all black and white, and some of the fancier ladies were wearing diamonds on their heads like Queen Elizabeth. The president of Austria came, and important senators and government officials, and ambassadors from around the world. All of Vienna was there to celebrate the return of their beloved Lipizzaners.

The orchestra swept into the opening bars of the waltz from *Der Rosenkavalier*, a gorgeous trumpeting burst of sound that made my ears prick up. "Dum da *dum* dum, dum dum *da-a-a-a-ah*," sang the French horns . . . and we were on.

I could feel Liesl vibrating like a humming-bird through the entire performance, but her hands on my reins were sure and steady. We shouldered into the pas de deux, dancing beside the Colonel and Pluto Theodorosta in perfect mirror image. I slid smoothly into the

piaffe when the time came, and Liesl sat still and upright and let me lead the way. Hans was right: I *did* know every step of every dance and, really, all she had to do was stay in the saddle. But she was better than that. When I leaped into my courbette we seemed to move as one. When I reared into the levade we looked just like the statue in front of the Hofburg—except it was Princess Eugénie on my back and not Prince Eugène! My girl was the best *Bereiter* of them all, if only for one night.

We made our final bow, and Liesl lifted the cocked hat off her shorn head with the traditional flourish. We left quickly and sped back to the Stallburg, where Liesl went to the supply closet and changed back into her dress. There was barely time. Within minutes the other horses and *Bereiter* were back. The stables filled with photographers and newspaper reporters and people raising glasses of champagne to toast our wonderful performance. The Colonel was surrounded all night by men slapping him on the back and ladies kissing him on the cheek. I didn't get to sleep until after midnight.

In all the excitement, no one seemed to notice that Liesl's braid was gone and Hans was limping. I think Martin suspected, but he never said a word.

As far as I know, Liesl and Hans never told anyone. I never have, either . . . until now.

Home

I am old now, but I have been young. And I remember.

I remember the years of training that made me, step by careful step, into the perfectly mannered creature I became.

I remember war. I remember a sky turned

red with fire, and Liesl, who whispered soothing words into my pricking ears. I remember
the day she saved my life, and I galloped
down a mountain path like a wild Arabian
racing over desert sands. I remember the
soldiers from America, with their wide smiles
and loud voices, and how they clapped and
whistled when I danced for them.

I remember Petra, my mother, with her
dark loving eyes and warm muzzle. I remember Colonel Alois Podhajsky, the Colonel,
and how he cared for us and worked so hard.
I remember *Oberbereiter* Martin Haas, and
how patient and kind he was to a green horse
from the country. And I remember Anton,
who was my friend.

I remember the piaffe, fiery and slow and

solemn. I remember the levade and the courbette, the ancient and beautiful moves only Lipizzaner stallions can do. I remember the long years of exile, and the glorious return to the Winter Riding Hall with Liesl on my back, as light as a dandelion puff and trembling with joy as we bowed to the portrait of the emperor. I remember the music, lilting and lovely, and the warming sound of applause.

I am retired now. When your legs grow stiff and you can no longer rise into your levade with ease, the time has come. And so I was returned to the golden fields and sunny slopes of Piber, where my life began so many years ago. Every spring I see my new sons and daughters totter into the sunshine on legs as black and slender as mine once were. When summer comes, and we walk up the dusty road into the mountains to graze the high pastures, I watch them run and play and roll on their backs in a meadow dotted with white flowers. Will any of my sons, I wonder, be chosen to make the long journey to Vienna? Will they eat out of marble and learn to dance in a glittering white ballroom?

When the shadows grow long across the grass and it is time to go, I know there will be fresh straw waiting in my stall, where my name is over the door. The water will be clean and cool in the bucket, the oats will be sweet and crisp with never a speck of chaff, and maybe there will be an apple for dessert.

I am Maestoso Petra, and I remember. I remember it all.

APPENDIX

MORE ABOUT THE LIPIZZANER

Born to Dance

When the world-famous Lipizzaner stallions of the Spanish Riding School perform, it is magical. They are fairy-tale beautiful, with smooth white coats, large dark eyes, and the delicate heads of their Arabian ancestors. The riders in their elegant uniforms are solemn and serious, focused on the task at hand. The horses seem to float, silently and serenely,

through intricate patterns as graceful as *Swan Lake*—this *is* a ballet, and the hard work of rehearsal must never show. Behind each flaw-less move are years of training, and a tradition that goes back to ancient Greece: the dressage

moves of the haute école, the high school, were first described in *On Horsemanship*, a book written by Xenophon around 350 BC.

The Spanish Riding School has survived war, famine, and the Hapsburg Empire that founded it. The school only survived World War II because of the tireless efforts of Colonel Alois Podhajsky, who was its director from 1939 to 1965. "We must live for the school," he wrote in his memoirs. "Offer our lives to it. Then perhaps, little by little, the light will grow from the tiny candle we keep lit here, and the great art—of the *haute école*—will not be snuffed out."

September 9, 2008, marked a turning point in the long history of the Spanish Riding School. On that day, a twenty-one-year-old

Austrian woman and a seventeen-year-old British woman began their training as riders! No woman had ridden in the beautiful Winter Riding Hall for over a century, not since ladies of the Imperial Court had been allowed to participate in riding festivals.

A Long History

The first Lipizzaners date from around AD 800, when desert horses from North Africa were brought to Spain and crossed with native Spanish horses. The new breed was sturdy, intelligent, and agile. By the sixteenth century the horses were in great demand, both for military uses and for the riding academies that had become fashionable among

European royalty. In 1580 the archduke Charles II, brother of the Austrian emperor Maximilian II, established a stud at Lipizza, in Slovenia, which gave the breed its name. In 1735 Emperor Charles VI founded the Spanish Riding School in Vienna, named it for the horses' country of origin, and built the Winter Riding Hall in the Imperial Palace.

The Federal Stud at Piber was established as the official source of the breed in 1920. Only the finest stallions and mares— those who display the best physical and mental qualities of the breed—are allowed to produce foals. All true Lipizzaners can trace their ancestry to one of six stallions: Pluto (born in 1765), Conversano (born in 1767), Neapolitano (born in 1790), Favory (born in 1779), Siglavy (born in 1810), and Maestoso (born in 1773). Mares are given only one name. Stallions are given two. The first is for the lineage of their sire, and the second is for their dam: Maestoso Petra, Conversano Nina, Pluto Theodorosta, etc.

"Airs Above the Ground"

Lipizzaners are compact—they stand between 15 and 16.1 hands—and extremely muscular, with powerful hindquarters that enable them to perform the "airs above the ground" for which they are famous. (The stallions' center of gravity is also further back than that of other breeds, which means they can stand on their hind legs without tiring.) These amazing moves, which no other breed can do, include the levade, in which the horse strikes a rearing pose and holds it; the courbette, in which the horse balances on his hind legs before hopping forward; the capriole, a jump in place

during which the horse kicks out his hind legs in midair; and the croupade, in which the horse jumps up and tucks all four legs under his body. These difficult moves grew out of dressage—not, as legend has it, from evasive tactics used in battle. Most Lipizzaners can perfect only two moves during their careers.

Taking Their Time

Lipizzaners live a very long time. It is not unusual for them to perform well into their twenties and live well into their thirties. Like Maestoso Petra, most stallions of the Spanish Riding School perform until they are about twenty-three years old, and then retire to stud. Everything takes time with these noble creatures: they are born coal black and it can take as long as five or six years for their coats to fade to white. They are not ready to begin training until they are four, and they are not considered fully mature until they are seven. The training to perform in the Spanish Riding School exhibitions is gentle and gradual and takes six years to complete. When their time in the spotlight has ended, these majestic horses live out their days in comfort, honored as elder statesmen and national treasures.

❧ COMING SOON! ❧

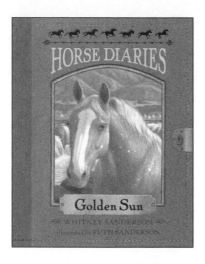

Oregon, 1790

Golden Sun is a chestnut snowflake Appaloosa. In summer, he treks through the mountains with his rider, a Nez Perce boy named Little Turtle, as he gathers healing plants. But when Little Turtle's best friend falls ill, Golden Sun discovers his true calling. Here is Golden Sun's story . . . in his own words.

About the Author

Jane Kendall is the author of the critically acclaimed historical novels *Miranda and the Movies* (which was a Junior Library Guild Selection for Advanced Readers) and *Miranda Goes to Hollywood* and the serialized time-travel fantasy *All in Good Time*. She has also illustrated more than two dozen children's books, including *The Nutcracker: A Ballet Cut-out Book*, Laurie Lawlor's Heartland series, and *The Alligator in the Closet* by David L. Harrison.

Ms. Kendall lives in Greenwich, Connecticut, and has been a senior writer for *Greenwich* magazine since 1992. She has written for the *New York Times* on film history, currently teaches a college-level writing course for the Institute of Children's Literature, and collects vintage hats (which she wears!). She was an enthusiastic rider growing up, and on one memorable occasion went Christmas caroling on horseback. "Give me a crisp New England fall day," she says, "and I still long for a chestnut horse and a quiet trail through the woods."

About the Illustrator

Ruth Sanderson grew up with a love for horses. She drew them constantly, and her first oil painting, at age fourteen, was a horse portrait.

Ruth has illustrated and retold many fairy tales and likes to feature horses in them whenever possible. Her book about a magical horse, *The Golden Mare, the Firebird, and the Magic Ring,* won the Texas Bluebonnet Award in 2003. She illustrated the first Black Stallion paperback covers and a number of chapter books about horses, most recently *Summer Pony* and *Winter Pony* by Jean Slaughter Doty.

Ruth and her daughter have two horses, an Appaloosa named Thor and a quarter horse named Gabriel. She lives with her family in Massachusetts.

To find out more about her adventures with horses and the research she did to create the illustrations in this book, visit her Web site, www.ruthsanderson.com.

Collect all the books in the
Horse Diaries series!

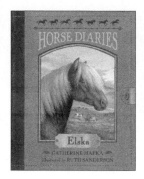

Elska

CATHERINE HAPKA
illustrated by RUTH SANDERSON

Bell's Star

ALISON HART
illustrated by RUTH SANDERSON

Koda

PATRICIA HERMES
illustrated by RUTH SANDERSON

And coming soon

Maestoso Petra

JANE KENDALL
illustrated by RUTH SANDERSON

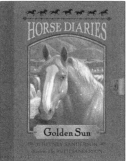

Golden Sun

WHITNEY SANDERSON
illustrated by RUTH SANDERSON